Welcome to Rider Nation!

_____

The ALWAYS Team
Trouble in Riderville

Written by Holly Preston
Illustrated by Val Lawton

Always  Books

The Always Team: Trouble in Riderville

Manufactured by Friesens Corporation in Altona, MB, Canada
September 2011
Job #66514

Library and Archives Canada Cataloguing in Publication

Preston, Holly
    The Always Team trouble in Riderville / written by Holly Preston ; illustrated by Val Lawton.

ISBN 978-0-9869244-0-8

    1. Saskatchewan Roughriders (Football team)--Juvenile fiction.
I. Lawton, Val, 1962- II. Title.

PS8631.R467A789 2011   jC813'.6   C2011-904958-9

Layout by Heather Nickel

With many thanks to the Saskatchewan Roughriders for their cooperation and support.

ENVIRONMENTAL BENEFITS STATEMENT

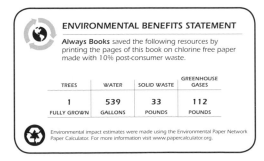

Always Books saved the following resources by printing the pages of this book on chlorine free paper made with 10% post-consumer waste.

TREES	WATER	SOLID WASTE	GREENHOUSE GASES
1	539	33	112
FULLY GROWN	GALLONS	POUNDS	POUNDS

Environmental impact estimates were made using the Environmental Paper Network Paper Calculator. For more information visit www.papercalculator.org.

MIX
Paper from responsible sources
FSC® C016245
www.fsc.org

www.thealwaysteam.com

For all young Rider fans who will grow up to be
great ambassadors for their team

The Rae Street Riders were having an awesome season.

It seemed they were **ALWAYS** winning.

Brendan, Rob and Stevie were the most improved football team
in the neighbourhood …

"Thanks to all we learned from the **ALWAYS** team," said Brendan.

"Rob, you're the best lineman I've ever played with," Stevie **ALWAYS** said.
"Stevie, you're the best receiver I've ever played with," Rob **ALWAYS** said.
Brendan believed he would **ALWAYS** be their star quarterback.

And they weren't the only team in town having a great season.
This year the **ALWAYS** Team was the best in the West!

Everything was perfect in Riderville.

At least, it seemed that way … until the day it wasn't perfect at all.

The best quarterback they ever had was moving!
It was **ALWAYS** hard to find a new quarterback — and even harder to replace a friend.
"Why do things **ALWAYS** have to change?" asked Rob.

Someone special **ALWAYS** had the recipe to cheer them up.

"Boys, have a treat, then get a good sleep," Grandma said.

"Tomorrow we're going to a Rider game."

Rob and Stevie knew that Grandma was right.
They **ALWAYS** had fun at Rider games.

Maybe it's because the players are **ALWAYS** awesome.

Maybe it's because the fans **ALWAYS** show their Rider Pride.

And maybe it's because the boys can **ALWAYS** count on Gainer
to make them laugh out loud!

"I'm sad Brendan's moving," said Stevie, "but I'm feeling a little better."
It was a feeling that wouldn't last long.

There was trouble in Riderville.

"Remember, boys," said Grandma, "the players on the bench are **ALWAYS** ready
to show what they can do." Grandma knew a lot about football.
She'd been a Rider fan forever.

And the players WERE up to the challenge! Every one of them. Except for one.
The team's kicker was hurt…and the backup was missing!
There could be no joy in Riderville.

"It's time for action!" Rob said. The boys had to help the team.
And soon they had a plan.

And that plan was — Gainer! Rider Nation's favourite gopher had learned not to kick visiting mascots anymore, but the boys were sure he could **ALWAYS** kick if he needed to. And he needed to now! They ran to find Gainer after the game.

Practice makes a gopher perfect!

Soon, the time for practice was over. It was the day of the Western Final.
The season was on the line. As **ALWAYS**, the Riders were playing their best.

The score was SO close. And before long, it was the last play of the game.
Rider fans know it **ALWAYS** comes down to this. It would take a field goal to win
… but who could they count on?

Rob and Stevie and all the Rider fans got the ending they'd **ALWAYS** wanted. And Grandma said, "Boys, your idea makes *you* heros, too!" They all hoped the starting kicker's foot would be better for the next game — the Grey Cup!

And Gainer could go back to being what he **ALWAYS** wanted to be,
the best mascot ever. Besides, Gainer knew the 13th man
ALWAYS belongs in the stands!

Rob and Stevie were happy as they walked home from Grandma's.
It had been a great day for football — except the Rae Street Riders
still didn't have a quarterback … or did they?

"What an arm!" the boys shouted together.
Even a perfect day in Riderville can **ALWAYS** get better!

Holly has been a Rider fan since way back when. Thankfully, her parents raised her in a place where green and white and community are words that ALWAYS belong in the same sentence.

She has had a career as a broadcast journalist with CTV and CBC. On the day our team brought the Grey Cup home in 1989, she was lucky to host a TV special from Taylor Field watched by fans throughout Saskatchewan. It's the only time she'll ever get to be on the 50-yard line. How sweet it was!

Today, Holly's two sons wear their Rider colours with pride, just as their grandfathers Ken and Ted would want.

Holly Preston

When you're a little girl growing up on the golden prairies of Saskatchewan, your dreams are as big as the endless swaying wheat fields and the eternal blue sky stretching overhead. For Val, those dreams were filled with simple, yet compelling images of people dotted against a landscape washed with sun.

While Val enjoys creating art for both kids' and grown-ups' books, she also loves working with schoolchildren as an artist-educator with the Royal Conservatory of Canada's "Learning Through the Arts" program.

Val lives with her husband, two kids and a beagle, all of whom cheer for the ALWAYS Team on game day!

Val Lawton